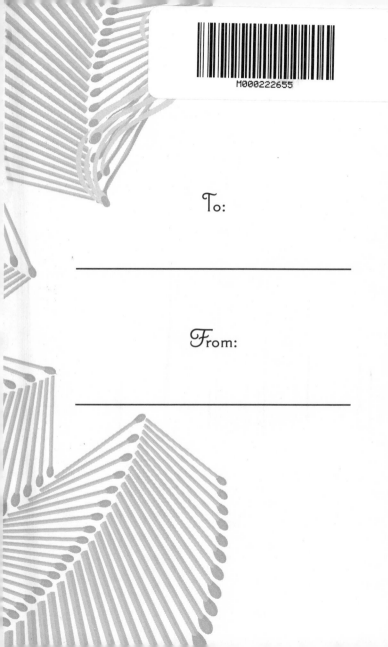

To:

_____

From:

_____

CHRISTMAS

with

Hans Christian Andersen

CHRISTMAS

with

Hans Christian Andersen

U

UNION
SQUARE
& CO.

NEW YORK

UNION SQUARE & CO.

NEW YORK

UNION SQUARE & CO. and the distinctive Union Square & Co. logo are
trademarks of Sterling Publishing Co., Inc.

Union Square & Co., LLC, is a subsidiary of Sterling Publishing Co., Inc.

ISBN 978-1-4549-4701-1
ISBN 978-1-4549-4730-1 (e-book)

For information about custom editions, special sales, and premium purchases,
please contact specialsales@unionsquareandco.com.

Printed in the United States

2 4 6 8 10 9 7 5 3

unionsquareandco.com

Interior design by Rich Hazelton

Contents

The Fir-Tree

O ut in the woods stood a nice little Fir-
tree. The place he had was a very good
one: the sun shone on him; as to fresh
air, there was enough of that, and round him grew
many large-sized comrades, pines as well as firs.
But the little Fir wanted so very much to be a
grown-up tree.

He did not think of the warm sun and of
the fresh air; he did not care for the little cottage-
children that ran about and prattled when they
were in the woods looking for wild strawberries.
The children often came with a whole pitcher full
of berries, or a long row of them threaded on a
straw, and sat down near the young tree and said,

"Oh, how pretty he is! what a nice little Fir!" But this was what the Tree could not bear to hear.

At the end of a year he had shot up a good deal, and after another year he was another long bit taller; for with fir-trees one can always tell by the shoots how many years old they are.

"Oh! were I but such a high tree as the others are," sighed he. "Then I should be able to spread out my branches, and with the tops to look into the wide world! Then would the birds build nests among my branches; and when there was a breeze, I could bend with as much stateliness as the others!"

Neither the sunbeams, nor the birds, nor the red clouds which morning and evening sailed above him, gave the little Tree any pleasure.

In winter, when the snow lay glittering on the ground, a hare would often come leaping along, and jump right over the little Tree. Oh, that made him so angry! But two winters were past, and in the third the Tree was so large that the hare was obliged to go round it. "To grow and grow, to get older and be tall," thought the Tree,—"that, after all, is the most delightful thing in the world!"

In autumn the wood-cutters always came and felled some of the largest trees. This happened every year; and the young Fir-tree, that had now grown to a very comely size, trembled at the sight; for the magnificent great trees fell to the earth with noise and cracking, the branches were lopped off, and the trees looked long and bare: they were hardly to be recognized; and then they were laid in carts, and the horses dragged them out of the wood.

Where did they go to? What became of them?

In spring, when the Swallows and the Storks came, the Tree asked them: "Don't you know where they have been taken? Have you not met them any where?"

The Swallows did not know anything about it; but the Stork looked musing, nodded his head, and said, "Yes; I think I know; I met many ships as I was flying hither from Egypt; on the ships were magnificent masts, and I venture to assert that it was they that smelt so of fir. I may congratulate you, for they lifted themselves on high most majestically!"

"Oh, were I but old enough to fly across the sea! But how does the sea look in reality? What is it like?"

"That would take a long time to explain," said the Stork, and with these words off he went.

"Rejoice in thy growth!" said the Sunbeams, "rejoice in thy vigorous growth, and in the fresh life that moveth within thee!"

And the Wind kissed the Tree, and the Dew wept tears over him; but the Fir understood it not.

When Christmas came, quite young trees were cut down; trees which often were not even as large or of the same age as this Fir-tree, who could never rest, but always wanted to be off. These young trees, and they were always the finest looking, retained their branches; they were laid on carts, and the horses drew them out of the wood.

"Where are they going to?" asked the Fir. "They are not taller than I; there was one indeed that was considerably shorter;—and why do they retain all their branches? Whither are they taken?"

"We know! we know!" chirped the Sparrows. "We have peeped in at the windows in the town below! We know whither they are taken! The greatest splendor and the greatest magnificence one can imagine await them. We peeped through the windows, and saw them planted in the middle of the warm room and ornamented with the most splendid things, with gilded apples, with gingerbread, with toys, and many hundred lights!"

"And then?" asked the Fir-tree, trembling in every bough. "And then? What happens then?"

"We did not see anything more; it was incomparably beautiful."

"I would fain know if I am destined for so glorious a career," cried the Tree, rejoicing. "That is still better than to cross the sea! What a longing do I suffer! Were Christmas but come! I am now tall, and my branches spread like the others that were carried off last year! Oh! were I but already on the cart! Were I in the warm room with all the splendor and magnificence! Yes; then something better, something still grander, will surely follow, or wherefore should they thus ornament me? Something better, something still grander, *must* follow—but what? Oh, how I long, how I suffer! I do not know myself what is the matter with me!"

"Rejoice in our presence!" said the Air and the Sunlight; "rejoice in thy own fresh youth!"

But the Tree did not rejoice at all; he grew and grew, and was green both winter and summer. People that saw him said, "What a fine tree!" and towards Christmas he was one of the first that was cut down. The axe struck deep into the very pith; the Tree fell to the earth with a sigh: he felt a pang—it was like a swoon; he could not think of happiness, for he was sorrowful at being separated from his home, from the place where he had sprung up. He well knew that he should never see his dear old comrades, the little bushes and flowers around him, any more; perhaps not even the birds! The departure was not at all agreeable.

The Tree only came to himself when he was unloaded in a court-yard with the other trees, and heard a man say, "That one is splendid! we don't want the others." Then two servants came in rich livery and carried the Fir-tree into a large and splendid drawing-room. Portraits were hanging on the walls, and near the white porcelain stove stood two large Chinese vases with lions on the covers. There, too, were large easy-chairs, silken sofas, large tables full of picture-books and full of toys, worth hundreds and hundreds of crowns— at least the children said so. And the Fir-tree was stuck upright in a cask that was filled with sand; but no one could see that it was a cask, for green cloth was hung all round it, and it stood on a large gaily-colored carpet. Oh! how the Tree quivered! What was to happen? The servants, as well as the young ladies, decorated it. On one branch there hung little nets cut out of colored paper, and each net was filled with sugar-plums; and among the other boughs gilded apples and walnuts were suspended, looking as though they had grown there, and little blue and white tapers were placed among the leaves. Dolls that looked for all the world like men—the Tree had never beheld such before— were seen among the foliage, and at the very top a large star of gold tinsel was fixed. It was really splendid—beyond description splendid.

"This evening!" they all said; "how it will shine this evening!"

"Oh!" thought the Tree, "if the evening were but come! If the tapers were but lighted! And then I wonder what will happen! Perhaps the other trees from the forest will come to look at me! Perhaps the sparrows will beat against the window-panes! I wonder if I shall take root here, and winter and summer stand covered with ornaments!"

He knew very much about the matter! But he was so impatient that for sheer longing he got a pain in his back, and this with trees is the same thing as a headache with us.

The candles were now lighted—What brightness! What splendor! The Tree trembled so in every bough that one of the tapers set fire to the foliage. It blazed up famously.

"Help! help!" cried the young ladies, and they quickly put out the fire.

Now the Tree did not even dare tremble. What a state he was in! He was so uneasy lest he should lose something of his splendor, that he was quite bewildered amidst the glare and brightness; when suddenly both folding-doors opened and a troop of children rushed in as if they would upset the Tree. The older persons followed quietly; the little ones stood quite still. But it was only for a moment; then they shouted that the whole place re-echoed with their rejoicing; they danced round the Tree, and one present after the other was pulled off.

"What are they about?" thought the Tree. "What is to happen now!" And the lights burned down to the very branches, and as they burned down they were put out one after the other, and then the children had permission to plunder the Tree. So they fell upon it with such violence that all its branches cracked; if it had not been fixed firmly in the ground, it would certainly have tumbled down.

The children danced about with their beautiful playthings: no one looked at the Tree except the old nurse, who peeped between the branches; but it was only to see if there was a fig or an apple left that had been forgotten.

"A story! a story!" cried the children, drawing a little fat man towards the Tree. He seated himself under it and said, "Now we are in the shade, and the Tree can listen too. But I shall tell only one story. Now which will you have; that about Ivedy-Avedy, or about Humpy-Dumpy, who tumbled down stairs, and yet after all came to the throne and married the princess?"

"Ivedy-Avedy," cried some; "Humpy-Dumpy," cried the others. There was such a bawling and screaming!—the Fir-tree alone was silent, and he thought to himself, "Am I not to bawl with the rest?—am I to do nothing whatever?" for he was one of the company, and had done what he had to do.

And the man told about Humpy-Dumpy that tumbled down, who notwithstanding came to the throne, and at last married the princess. And the children clapped their hands, and cried. "Oh, go on! Do go on!" They wanted to hear about Ivedy-Avedy too, but the little man only told them about Humpy-Dumpy. The Fir-tree stood quite still and absorbed in thought: the birds in the wood had never related the like of this. "Humpy-Dumpy fell down stairs, and yet he married the princess! Yes, yes! that's the way of the world!" thought the Fir-tree, and believed it all, because the man who told the story was so good-looking. "Well, well! who knows, perhaps I may fall down stairs, too, and get a princess as wife!" And he looked forward with joy to the morrow, when he hoped to be decked out again with lights, playthings, fruits, and tinsel.

"I won't tremble to-morrow!" thought the Fir-tree. "I will enjoy to the full all my splendor! To-morrow I shall hear again the story of Humpy-Dumpy, and perhaps that of Ivedy-Avedy too." And the whole night the Tree stood still and in deep thought.

In the morning the servant and the housemaid came in.

"Now then the splendor will begin again," thought the Fir. But they dragged him out of the room, and up the stairs into the loft: and here, in a dark corner, where no daylight could enter, they left him. "What's the meaning of this?" thought the Tree. "What am I to do here? What shall I hear now, I wonder?" And he leaned against the wall lost in reverie. Time enough had he too for his reflections; for days and nights passed on, and nobody came up; and when at last somebody did come, it was only to put some great trunks in a corner, out of the way. There stood the Tree quite hidden; it seemed as if he had been entirely forgotten.

"'Tis now winter out of doors!" thought the Tree. "The earth is hard and covered with snow;

men cannot plant me now, and therefore I have been put up here under shelter till the spring-time comes! How thoughtful that is! How kind man is, after all! If it only were not so dark here, and so terribly lonely! Not even a hare!—And out in the woods it was so pleasant, when the snow was on the ground, and the hare leaped by; yes—even when he jumped over me; but I did not like it then! It is really terribly lonely here!"

"Squeak! squeak!" said a little Mouse, at the same moment, peeping out of his hole. And then another little one came. They snuffed about the Fir-tree, and rustled among the branches.

"It is dreadfully cold," said the Mouse. "But for that, it would be delightful here, old Fir, wouldn't it?"

"I am by no means old," said the Fir-tree. "There's many a one considerably older than I am."

"Where do you come from," asked the Mice, "and what can you do?" They were so extremely curious. "Tell us about the most beautiful spot on the earth. Have you never been there? Were you never in the larder, where cheeses lie on the shelves, and hams hang from above; where one dances about on tallow candles; that place where one enters lean, and comes out again fat and portly?"

"I know no such place," said the Tree. "But I know the wood, where the sun shines and where the little birds sing." And then he told all about his youth; and the little Mice had never heard the like before; and they listened and said,

"Well, to be sure! How much you have seen! How happy you must have been!"

"I!" said the Fir-tree, thinking over what he had himself related. "Yes, in reality those were happy times." And then he told about Christmas-eve, when he was decked out with cakes and candles.

"Oh," said the little Mice, "how fortunate you have been, old Fir-tree!"

"I am by no means old," said he. "I came from the wood this winter; I am in my prime, and am only rather short for my age."

"What delightful stories you know!" said the Mice: and the next night they came with four other little Mice, who were to hear what the Tree recounted; and the more he related, the more plainly he remembered all himself; and it appeared as if those times had really been happy times. "But they may still come—they may still come! Humpy-Dumpy fell down stairs, and yet he got a princess!" and he thought at the moment of a nice little Birch-tree growing out in the woods: to the Fir, that would be a real charming princess.

"Who is Humpy-Dumpy?" asked the Mice. So then the Fir-tree told the whole fairy tale, for he could remember every single word of it; and the little Mice jumped for joy up to the very top of the Tree. Next night two more Mice came, and on Sunday two Rats even; but they said the stories were not interesting, which vexed the little Mice; and they, too, now began to think them not so very amusing either.

"Do you know only one story?" asked the Rats.

"Only that one," answered the Tree. "I heard it on my happiest evening; but I did not then know how happy I was."

"It is a very stupid story! Don't you know one about bacon and tallow candles? Can't you tell any larder-stories?"

"No," said the Tree.

"Then good-bye," said the Rats; and they went home.

At last the little Mice stayed away also; and the Tree sighed: "After all, it was very pleasant when the sleek little Mice sat round me and listened to what I told them. Now that too is over. But I will take good care to enjoy myself when I am brought out again."

But when was that to be? Why, one morning there came a quantity of people and set to work in the loft. The trunks were moved, the tree was pulled out and thrown—rather hard, it is true,—down on the floor, but a man drew him towards the stairs, where the daylight shone.

"Now a merry life will begin again," thought the Tree. He felt the fresh air, the first sunbeam,— and now he was out in the court-yard. All passed so quickly, there was so much going on around him, the Tree quite forgot to look to himself. The court adjoined a garden, and all was in flower; the roses hung so fresh and odorous over the balustrade, the lindens were in blossom, the Swallows flew by, and said, "Quirre-vit! my husband is come!" but it was not the Fir-tree that they meant.

"Now, then, I shall really enjoy life," said he exultingly, and spread out his branches; but, alas! they were all withered and yellow! It was in a corner that he lay, among weeds and nettles. The golden star of tinsel was still on the top of the Tree, and glittered in the sunshine.

In the court-yard some of the merry children were playing who had danced at Christmas round the Fir-tree, and were so glad at the sight of him. One of the youngest ran and tore off the golden star.

"Only look what is still on the ugly old Christmas tree!" said he, trampling on the branches, so that they all cracked beneath his feet.

And the Tree beheld all the beauty of the flowers, and the freshness in the garden; he beheld himself, and wished he had remained in his dark corner in the loft: he thought of his first youth in the wood, of the merry Christmas-eve, and of the little Mice who had listened with so much pleasure to the story of Humpy-Dumpy.

"'Tis over! 'Tis past!" said the poor Tree. "Had I but rejoiced when I had reason to do so! But now 'tis past, 'tis past!"

And the gardener's boy chopped the Tree into small pieces; there was a whole heap lying there. The wood flamed up splendidly under the large brewing copper, and it sighed so deeply! Each sigh was like a shot.

The boys played about in the court, and the youngest wore the gold star on his breast which the Tree had had on the happiest evening of his life. However, that was over now,—the Tree gone, the story at an end. All, all was over;—every tale must end at last.

The Snow Man

It is so wonderfully cold that my whole body crackles!" said the Snow Man. "This is a kind of wind that can blow life into one; and how the gleaming one up yonder is staring at me." This was the sun he meant, which was just about to set. "It shall not make *me* wink—I shall manage to keep the pieces."

He had two triangular pieces of tile in his head instead of eyes. His mouth was made of an old rake, and consequently was furnished with teeth.

He had been born amid the joyous shouts of the boys, and welcomed by the sound of sledge-bells and the slashing of whips.

The sun went down and the full moon rose, round, large, clear, and beautiful in the blue air.

"There it comes again from the other side," said the Snow Man. He intended to say the sun is showing himself again. "Ah! I have cured him of staring. Now let him hang up there and shine that I may see myself. If I only knew how I could manage to move from this place I should like so much to move. If I could I would slide along yonder on the ice, just as I see the boys slide; but I don't understand it; I don't know how to run."

"Away! away!" barked the old Yard Dog. He was quite hoarse and could not pronounce the genuine "Bow, bow." He had got the hoarseness from the time when he was an indoor dog and lay by the fire. "The sun will teach you to run! I saw that last winter in your predecessor, and before that in *his* predecessor. Away! away! and away they all go."

"I don't understand you, comrade," said the Snow Man. "That thing up yonder is to teach me to run?" He meant the moon. "Yes, it was running itself when I saw it a little while ago, and now it comes creeping from the other side."

"You know nothing at all," retorted the Yard Dog. "But then you've only just been patched up.

What you see yonder is the moon, and the one that went before was the sun. It will come again to-morrow and will teach you to run down into the ditch by the wall. We shall soon have a change of weather; I can feel that in my left hind leg, for it pricks and pains me—the weather is going to change."

"I don't understand him," said the Snow Man; "but I have a feeling that he's talking about something disagreeable. The one who stared so just now, and whom he called the sun, is not my friend. I can feel that."

"Away! away!" barked the Yard Dog; and he turned round three times and then crept into his kennel to sleep.

The weather really changed. Toward morning a thick, damp fog lay over the whole region; later there came a wind, an icy wind. The cold seemed quite to seize upon one; but when the sun rose what splendor! Trees and bushes were covered with hoarfrost and looked like a complete forest of coral, and every twig seemed covered with gleaming white buds. The many delicate ramifications, concealed in summer by the wreath of leaves, now made their appearance; it seemed like a lace-work gleaming white. A snowy radiance sprang from every twig. The birch waved in the wind—it had life like the rest of the trees in summer. It was wonderfully beautiful. And when the sun shone, how it all gleamed and sparkled, as if diamond dust had been strewn everywhere and big dia-monds had been dropped on the snowy carpet of the earth! Or one could imagine that countless little lights were gleaming whiter than even the snow itself.

"That is wonderfully beautiful," said a young girl who came with a young man into the garden. They both stood still near the Snow Man and contemplated the glittering trees. "Summer cannot show a more beautiful sight," said she; and her eyes sparkled.

"And we can't have such a fellow as this in summer-time," replied the young man, and he pointed to the Snow Man. "He is capital."

The girl laughed, nodded to the Snow Man, and then danced away over the snow with her friend—over the snow that cracked and crackled under her tread as if she were walking on starch.

"Who were those two?" the Snow Man inquired of the Yard Dog. "You've been longer in the yard than I. Do you know them?"

"Of course I know them," replied the Yard Dog. "She has stroked me, and he has thrown me a meat-bone. I don't bite those two.

"But what are they?" asked the Snow Man.

"Lovers!" replied the Yard Dog. "They will go to live in the same kennel and gnaw at the same bone. Away! away!"

"Are they the same kind of beings as you and I?" asked the Snow Man.

"Why, they belong to the master!" retorted the Yard Dog. "People certainly know very little who were only born yesterday. I can see that in you. I have age and information. I know every one here in the house, and I know a time when I did not lie out here in the cold fastened to a chain. Away! away!"

"The cold is charming," said the Snow Man. "Tell me, tell me. But you must not clank your chain, for it jars within me when you do that."

"Away! away!" barked the Yard Dog. "They told me I was a pretty little fellow; then I used to lie in a chair covered with velvet up in master's house, and sit in the lap of the mistress of all. They used to kiss my nose and wipe my paws with an embroidered hand-kerchief. I was called 'Ami—dear Ami—sweet Ami.' But afterward I grew too big for them, and they gave me away to the housekeeper. So I came to live in the basement story. You can look into that from where you are standing, and you can see into the room where I was master; for I was master at the housekeeper's. It was certainly a smaller place than up-stairs, but I was more comfortable, and was not continually taken hold of and pulled about by children as I had been. I received just as much good food as ever, and even better. I had my own cushion, and there was a stove, the finest thing in the world at this season. I went under the stove, and could lie down quite beneath it. Ah! I still sometimes dream of that stove. Away! away!"

"Does a stove look so beautiful?" asked the Snow Man. "Is it at all like me?"

"It's just the reverse of you. It's as black as a crow, and has a long neck and a brazen drum. It eats firewood so that the fire spurts out of its mouth. One must keep at its side or under it, and there one is very comfortable. You can see it through the window from where you stand."

And the Snow Man looked and saw a bright, polished thing with a brazen drum, and the fire gleamed from the lower part of it. The Snow Man felt quite strangely; an odd emotion came over him; he knew not what it meant and could not account for it; but all people who are not snow men know the feeling.

"And why did you leave her?" asked the Snow Man, for it seemed to him that the stove must be of the female sex. "How could you quit such a comfortable place?"

"I was obliged," replied the Yard Dog. "They turned me out of doors and chained me up here. I had bitten the youngest young master in the leg because he kicked away the bone I was gnawing. 'Bone for bone,' I thought. They took that very much amiss, and from that time I have been fastened to a chain and have lost my voice. Don't you hear how hoarse I am? Away! away! I can't talk any more like other dogs. Away! away! That was the end of the affair."

But the Snow Man was no longer listening to him. He was looking in at the housekeeper's basement lodging, into the room where the stove stood on its four iron legs, just the same size as the Snow Man himself.

"What a strange crackling within me!" he said. "Shall I ever get in there? It is an innocent wish, and our innocent wishes are certain to be fulfilled. I must go in there and lean against her, even if I have to break through the window."

"You'll never get in there," said the Yard Dog; "and if you approach the stove you'll melt away—away!"

"I am as good as gone," replied the Snow Man. "I think I am breaking up."

The whole day the Snow Man stood looking in through the window. In the twilight hour the room became still more inviting; from the stove came a mild gleam, not like the sun nor like the moon; no, it was only as the stove can glow when he has something to eat. When the room door opened the flame started out of his mouth; this was a habit the stove had. The flame fell distinctly on the white face of the Snow Man and gleamed red upon his bosom.

"I can endure it no longer," said he. "How beautiful it looks when it stretches out its tongue!"

The night was long; but it did not appear long to the Snow Man, who stood there lost in his own charming reflections, crackling with the cold.

In the morning the window-panes of the basement lodging were covered with ice. They bore the most beautiful ice flowers that any snow man could desire; but they concealed the stove. The window-panes would not thaw; he could not see the stove, which he pictured to himself as a lovely female. It crackled and whistled in him and around him; it was just the kind of frosty weather a snow man must thoroughly enjoy.

But he did not enjoy it; and, indeed, how could he enjoy himself when he was stove-sick?

"That's a terrible disease for a Snow Man," said the Yard Dog. "I have suffered from it myself, but I got over it. Away! away!" he barked; and he added, "The weather is going to change."

And the weather did change; it began to thaw. The warmth increased, and the Snow Man decreased. He made no complaint—and that's an infallible sign.

One morning he broke down. And, behold, where he had stood something like a broomstick remained sticking up out of the ground. It was the pole around which the boys had built him up.

"Ah! now I can understand why he had such an intense longing," said the Yard Dog. "Why, there's a shovel for cleaning out the stove fastened to the pole. The Snow Man had a stove-rake in his body, and that's what moved within him. Now he has got over that, too. Away! away!"

And soon they had got over the winter.

"Away! away!" barked the hoarse Yard Dog; but the girls in the house sang:

"Green thyme, from your house come out;
  Willow, your woolly fingers stretch out;
  Lark and cuckoo, cheerfully sing,
  For in February is coming the spring;
  And with the cuckoo I'll sing, too.
  Come thou, dear sun, come out, cuckoo!"

And nobody thought any more of the Snow Man.

The Little
Match-Girl

It was terribly cold; it snowed and was already almost dark, and evening came on, the last evening of the year. In the cold and gloom a poor little girl, bareheaded and barefoot, was walking through the streets. When she left her own house she certainly had had slippers on; but of what use were they? They were very big slippers, and her mother had used them till then, so big were they. The little maid lost them as she slipped across the road, where two carriages were rattling by terribly fast. One slipper was not to be found again, and a boy had seized the other and run away with it. He thought he could use it very well as a cradle some day when he had children of his own. So now the little girl went with her little naked feet, which were quite red and blue with the cold. In an old apron she carried a number of matches, and a bundle of them in her hand. No one had bought anything of her all day, and no one had given her a farthing.

Shivering with cold and hunger, she crept along, a picture of misery, poor little girl! The snowflakes covered her long fair hair, which fell in pretty curls over her neck; but she did not think of that now. In all the windows lights were shining, and there was a glorious smell of roast goose, for it was New-year's eve. Yes, she thought of that!

In a corner formed by two houses, one of which projected beyond the other, she sat down, cowering. She had drawn up her little feet, but she was still colder, and she did not dare to go home, for she had sold no matches and did not bring a farthing of money. From her father she would certainly receive a beating; and, besides, it was cold at home, for they had nothing over them but a roof through which the wind whistled, though the largest rents had been stopped with straw and rags.

Her little hands were almost benumbed with the cold. Ah, a match might do her good, if she could only draw one from the bundle and rub it against the wall and warm her hands at it. She drew one out. R-r-atch! how it sputtered and burned! It was a warm, bright flame, like a little candle, when she held her hands over it; it was a wonderful little light! It really seemed to the little girl as if she sat before a great polished stove with bright brass feet and a brass cover. How the fire burned! How comfortable it was! But the little flame went out, the stove vanished, and she had only the remains of the burnt match in her hand.

A second was rubbed against the wall. It burned up, and when the light fell upon the wall it became transparent like a thin veil, and she could see through it into the room. On the table a snow-white cloth was spread; upon it stood a shining dinner service; the roast goose smoked gloriously, stuffed with apples and dried plums. And, what was still more splendid to behold, the goose hopped down from the dish and waddled along the floor, with a knife and fork in its breast, to the little girl. Then the match went out and only the thick, damp, cold wall was before her. She lighted another match. Then she was sitting under a beautiful Christmas tree; it was greater and more ornamented than the one she had seen through the glass door at the rich merchant's. Thousands of candles burned upon the green branches, and colored pictures like those in the print-shops looked down upon them. The little girl stretched forth her hand toward them; then the match went out. The Christmas lights mounted higher. She saw them now as stars in the sky; one of them fell down, forming a long line of fire.

"Now some one is dying," thought the little girl, for her old grandmother, the only person who had loved her, and who was now dead, had told her that when a star fell down a soul mounted up to God.

She rubbed another match against the wall; it became bright again, and in the brightness the old grandmother stood clear and shining, mild and lovely.

"Grandmother!" cried the child. "Oh, take me with you! I know you will go when the match is burned out. You will vanish like the warm fire, the warm food, and the great, glorious Christmas tree!"

And she hastily rubbed the whole bundle of matches, for she wished to hold her grandmother fast. And the matches burned with such a glow that it became brighter than in the middle of the day; grandmother had never been so large or so beautiful. She took the little girl in her arms, and both flew in brightness and joy above the earth, very, very high, and up there was neither cold, nor hunger, nor care—they were with God.

But in the corner, leaning against the wall, sat the poor girl with red cheeks and smiling mouth, frozen to death on the last evening of the old year. The New-year's sun rose upon a little corpse! The child sat there, stiff and cold, with the matches, of which one bundle was burned. "She wanted to warm herself," the people said. No one imagined what a beautiful thing she had seen and in what glory she had gone in with her grandmother to the New-year's day.

The Last Dream
of the Old Oak

In the forest, high up on the steep shore, and not far from the open sea-coast, stood a very old oak-tree. It was just three hundred and sixty-five years old, but that long time was to the tree as the same number of days might be to us; we wake by day and sleep by night, and then we have our dreams. It is different with the tree; it is obliged to keep awake through three seasons of the year, and does not get any sleep till winter comes. Winter is its time for rest; its night after the long day of spring, summer, and autumn. On many a warm summer, the Ephemera, the flies that exist for only a day, had fluttered about the old oak, enjoyed life and felt happy and if, for a moment, one of the tiny creatures rested on one of his large fresh leaves, the tree would always say, "Poor little creature! your whole life consists only of a single day. How very short. It must be quite melancholy."

"Melancholy! what do you mean?" the little creature would always reply. "Everything around me is so wonderfully bright, and warm, and beautiful, that it makes me joyous."

"But only for one day, and then it is all over."

"Over!" repeated the fly; "what is the meaning of all over? Are you all over too?"

"No; I shall very likely live for thousands of your days, and my day is whole seasons long; indeed it is so long that you could never reckon it out."

"No? then I don't understand you. You may have thousands of my days, but I have thousands of moments in which I can be merry and happy. Does all the beauty of the world cease when you die?"

"No," replied the tree; "it will certainly last much longer,—infinitely longer than I can even think of."

"Well, then," said the little fly, "we have the same time to live; only we reckon differently." And the little creature danced and floated in the air, rejoicing in her delicate wings of gauze and velvet, rejoicing in the balmy breezes, laden with the fragrance of clover-fields and wild roses, elder-blossoms and honeysuckle, from the garden hedges, wild thyme, primroses, and mint, and the scent of all these was so strong that the perfume almost intoxicated the little fly. The long and beautiful day had been so full of joy and sweet delights, that when the sun sank low it felt tired of all its happiness and enjoyment. Its wings could sustain it no longer, and gently and slowly it glided down upon the soft waving blades of grass, nodded its little head as well as it could nod, and slept peacefully and sweetly. The fly was dead.

"Poor little Ephemera!" said the oak; "what a terribly short life!" And so, on every summer day the dance was repeated, the same questions asked, and the same answers given. The same thing was continued through many generations of Ephemera; all of them felt equally merry and equally happy.

The oak remained awake through the morning of spring, the noon of summer, and the evening of autumn; its time of rest, its night drew nigh—winter was coming. Already the storms were singing, "Good-night, good-night." Here fell a leaf and there fell a leaf. "We will rock you and lull you. Go to sleep, go to sleep. We will sing you to sleep, and shake you to sleep, and it will do your old twigs good; they will even crackle with pleasure. Sleep sweetly, sleep sweetly, it is your three-hundred-and-sixty-fifth night. Correctly speaking, you are but a youngster in the world. Sleep sweetly, the clouds will drop snow upon you, which will be quite a cover-lid, warm and sheltering to your feet. Sweet sleep to you, and pleasant dreams." And there stood the oak, stripped of all its leaves, left to rest during the whole of a long winter, and to dream many dreams of events that had happened in its life, as in the dreams of men. The great tree had once been small; indeed, in its cradle it had been an acorn. According to human computation, it was now in the fourth century of its existence. It was the largest and best tree in the forest. Its summit towered above all the other trees, and could be seen far out at sea, so that it served as a landmark to the sailors. It had no idea how many eyes looked eagerly for it. In its topmost branches the wood-pigeon built her nest, and the cuckoo carried out his usual vocal performances, and his well-known notes echoed amid the boughs; and in autumn, when the leaves looked like beaten copper plates, the birds of passage would come and rest upon the branches before taking their flight across the sea. But now it was winter, the tree stood leafless, so that every one could see how crooked and bent were the branches that sprang forth from the trunk. Crows and rooks came by turns and sat on them, and talked of the hard times which were beginning, and how difficult it was in winter to obtain food.

It was just about holy Christmas time that the tree dreamed a dream. The tree had, doubtless, a kind of feeling that the festive time had arrived, and in his dream fancied he heard the bells ringing from all the churches round, and yet it seemed to him to be a beautiful summer's day, mild and warm. His mighty summits was crowned with spreading fresh green foliage; the sunbeams played among the leaves and branches, and the air was full of fragrance from herb and blossom; painted butterflies chased each other; the summer flies danced around him, as if the world had been created merely for them to dance and be merry in. All that had happened to the tree during every year of his life seemed to pass before him, as in a festive procession. He saw the knights of olden times and noble ladies ride by through the wood on their gallant steeds, with plumes waving in their hats, and falcons on their wrists. The hunting horn sounded, and the dogs barked. He saw hostile warriors, in colored dresses and glittering armor, with spear and halberd, pitching their tents, and anon striking them. The watchfires again blazed, and men sang and slept under the hospitable shelter of the tree. He saw lovers meet in quiet happiness near him in the moonshine, and carve the initials of their names in the grayish-green bark on his trunk. Once, but long years had intervened since then, guitars and Eolian harps had been hung on his boughs by merry travellers; now they seemed to hang there again, and he could hear their marvellous tones. The wood-pigeons cooed as if to explain the feelings of the tree, and the cuckoo called out to tell him how many summer days he had yet to live. Then it seemed as if new life was thrilling through every fibre of root and stem and leaf, rising even to the highest branches. The tree felt itself stretching and spreading out, while through the root beneath the earth ran the warm vigor of life. As he grew higher and still higher, with increased strength, his topmost boughs became broader and fuller; and in proportion to his growth, so was his self-satisfaction increased, and with it arose a joyous longing to grow higher and higher, to reach even to the warm, bright sun itself. Already had his topmost branches pierced the clouds, which floated beneath them like troops of birds of passage, or large white swans; every leaf seemed gifted with sight, as if it possessed eyes to see. The stars became visible in broad daylight, large and sparkling, like clear and gentle eyes. They recalled to the memory the well-known look in the eyes of a child, or in the eyes of lovers who had once met beneath the branches of the old oak. These were wonderful and happy moments for the old tree, full of peace and joy; and yet, amidst all this happiness, the tree felt a yearning, longing desire that all the other trees, bushes, herbs, and flowers beneath him, might be able also to rise higher, as he had done, and to see all this splendor, and experience the same happiness. The grand, majestic oak could not be quite happy in the midst of his enjoyment, while all the rest, both great and small, were not with him. And this feeling of yearning trembled through every branch, through every leaf, as warmly and fervently as if they had been the fibres of a human heart. The summit of the tree waved to and fro, and bent downwards as if in his silent longing he sought for something. Then there came to him the fragrance of thyme, followed by the more powerful scent of honeysuckle and violets; and he fancied he heard the note of the cuckoo. At length his longing was satisfied. Up through the clouds came the green summits of the forest trees, and beneath him, the oak saw them rising, and growing higher and higher. Bush and herb shot upward, and some even tore themselves up by the roots to rise more quickly. The birch-tree was the quickest of all. Like a lightning flash the slender stem shot upwards in a zigzag line, the branches spreading around it like green gauze and banners. Every native of the wood, even to the brown and feathery rushes, grew with the rest, while the birds ascended with the melody of song. On a blade of grass, that fluttered in the air like a long-green ribbon, sat a grasshopper, cleaning his wings with his legs. May beetles hummed, the bees murmured, the birds sang, each in his own way; the air was filled with the sounds of song and gladness.

"But where is the little blue flower that grows by the water?" asked the oak, "and the purple bell-flower, and the daisy?" You see the oak wanted to have them all with him.

"Here we are, we are here," sounded in voice and song.

"But the beautiful thyme of last summer, where is that? and the lilies-of-the-valley, which last year covered the earth with their bloom? and the wild apple-tree with its lovely blossoms, and all the glory of the wood, which has flourished year after year? even what may have but now sprouted forth could be with us here."

"We are here, we are here," sounded voices higher in the air, as if they had flown there beforehand.

"Why this is beautiful, too beautiful to be believed," said the oak in a joyful tone. "I have them all here, both great and small; not one has been forgotten. Can such happiness be imagined?" It seemed almost impossible.

"In heaven with the Eternal God, it can be imagined, and it is possible," sounded the reply through the air.

And the old tree, as it still grew upwards and onwards, felt that his roots were loosening themselves from the earth.

"It is right so, it is best," said the tree, "no fetters hold me now. I can fly up to the very highest point in light and glory. And all I love are with me, both small and great. All—all are here."

Such was the dream of the old oak: and while he dreamed, a mighty storm came rushing over land and sea, at the holy Christmas time. The sea rolled in great billows towards the shore. There was a cracking and crushing heard in the tree. The root was torn from the ground just at the moment when in his dream he fancied it was being loosened from the earth. He fell—his three hundred and sixty-five years were passed as the single day of the Ephemera. On the morning of Christmas-day, when the sun rose, the storm had ceased. From all the churches sounded the festive bells, and from every hearth, even of the smallest hut, rose the smoke into the blue sky, like the smoke from the festive thank-offerings on the Druids' altars. The sea gradually became calm, and on board a great ship that had withstood the tempest during the night, all the flags were displayed, as a token of joy and festivity. "The tree is down! The old oak,—our landmark on the coast!" exclaimed the sailors. "It must have fallen in the storm of last night. Who can replace it? Alas! no one." This was a funeral oration over the old tree; short, but well-meant. There it lay stretched on the snow-covered shore, and over it sounded the notes of a song from the ship—a song of Christmas joy, and of the redemption of the soul of man, and of eternal life through Christ's atoning blood.

> "Sing aloud on the happy morn,
>   All is fulfilled, for Christ is born;
>   With songs of joy let us loudly sing,
>   'Hallelujahs to Christ our King.'"

Thus sounded the old Christmas carol, and every one on board the ship felt his thoughts elevated, through the song and the prayer, even as the old tree had felt lifted up in its last, its beautiful dream on that Christmas morn.

Signature Select Classics

Elegantly Designed Booklets of Poetry and Prose

This book is part of Union Square & Co.'s Signature Select Classics chapbook series. Each booklet features distinguished poetry and prose by the world's greatest poets and writers in an elegantly designed and printed chapbook binding. Compact and portable, they fit comfortably in the hand and can be carried conveniently anywhere. These books are essential reading for lovers of classic literature and collectible editions in their own right. They make perfect keepsakes to own and to share with others.